CONFESSIONS OF A
FORMER BULLY

CONFESSIONS OF A
FORMER BULLY

BY **Trudy Ludwig**
ILLUSTRATIONS BY **Beth Adams**

DRAGONFLY BOOKS

New York

A NOTE FROM Katie

A few months ago, I got sent to the principal's office again. Only this time, my parents were there waiting for me.

Mom looked like she'd just sucked a lemon.

Dad had steam coming out of his ears.

"Young lady, we need to talk," said Mr. Sanders. When the principal called me "young lady," I knew I was in BIG trouble.

Uh-oh, I remember thinking. *They must have found out what happened at morning recess.*

I was right. Some kids told Mrs. Patel, the playground monitor, that they saw me being really mean to Monica. And that it wasn't the first time.

"Well, Katie, what do you have to say for yourself?" asked Mr. Sanders.

I tried to figure out what I could say to get out of trouble. Nothing great came to mind. Telling grown-ups what they wanted to hear had worked for me before, so I ended up mumbling, "Sorry," even though I really wasn't.

Mom's shoe tapped on the floor. *Tap. Tap. Tap.*

Dad was giving me his famous Death Glare—staring right at me and through me at the same time.

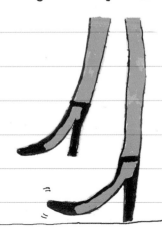

Mr. Sanders' sharp voice cut through the silence. "Katie, your bullying behavior is completely unacceptable here at Forest Heights Elementary."

"But I wasn't bullying," I said. "I didn't hit her or anything."

"Bullying isn't just about hurting someone with your hands," he said. "It's also about hurting with your words and behavior. And there are consequences for students who choose to bully others."

Consequences? I thought. *Uh-oh. That's definitely NOT a good word to hear from the principal!*

Mr. Sanders made me look it up in the dictionary.

con·se·quence \\'kän(t)-se-ˌkwen(t)s, -kwən(t)s\\ *n* (14c)
1: something that happens as a result of a particular action
2: a conclusion derived through logic : INFERENCE **3 a:**

Then he told me what the consequences were going to be for my bullying behavior. I called it my Had-To-Do-It-Whether-I-Liked-It-Or-Not List:

1. I had to spend three lunch periods in the principal's office, thinking about what I did wrong and writing down three ways I could have handled myself differently—without hurting anyone.

2. I had to meet with Mrs. Petrowski, the school counselor, once a week to learn more about "bullying behaviors" and how to be a better friend.

3. I had to figure out how to make up for the hurt I caused when I bullied other kids.

Sheesh! Those were some tough consequences.

It wasn't long before I checked Consequence #1 off the list. Consequence #2 didn't seem like it would be a big deal. But the last consequence was a whole different story. How was I going to check off Consequence #3?

At first, I was nervous about meeting with Mrs. Petrowski every Tuesday afternoon. But she actually turned out to be pretty cool for a grown-up. And I learned a lot—way more than I thought I would. My parents had me keep a journal to write down all the important stuff I was learning. I even included some of Mrs. Petrowski's Think About It and Quick Facts cards she gave me to help me think about bullying and friendships in a whole different way.

One day, when I was waiting for my mom to pick me up after school, Mrs. Petrowski noticed me writing in my journal. She asked if she could take a peek, and I let her. She smiled as she read some of the pages.

"You know, Katie," she said, "you've got a lot of helpful information in that journal of yours."

That's when it hit me: The Best Idea EVER! I finally came up with a great way to "right my wrong"—the last of Mr. Sanders' three consequences. I'd turn my journal into a special book for kids about bullying, so they could learn why it's not okay and what they could do to help stop it.

The next day, I met with Mr. Sanders and Mrs. Petrowski to talk about my idea. Guess what? **THEY LOVED IT!!** So that's the story behind this book. I'm excited that you're reading it. And I hope it'll help you like it helped me.

Sincerely,

Katie

THINK ABOUT IT

"As you grow older, you will discover that you have two hands, one for helping yourself, the other for helping others."

—SAM LEVENSON

MY VERY IMPORTANT BOOK

ABOUT BULLYING

by Katie

P-S-S-S-T!

I'm going to tell you what you need to know about bullying. I've even included stuff that kids who bully DON'T want you to find out. And believe me, I know what I'm talking about since I used to be one.

I stopped bullying with the help of our school counselor, Mrs. Petrowski. She must have spent a gazillion hours studying bullying because she knows so much about it. I never thought what I did to my friend Monica— giving her the silent treatment, telling her who she could be friends with, and not including her in games at recess—was bullying.

I was surprised to find out that it actually was.

One of the first things I learned was that bullying hurts everyone, even the kids who are bullying! That got me thinking: What's the point of doing something if it ends up hurting ME in the end?

I also noticed that while most kids at school had close friends, I didn't. Not having a best friend made me feel sad and lonely.

When I told Mrs. Petrowski how I felt, she went to her Think About It file and pulled out this card:

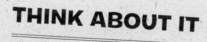

THINK ABOUT IT

"My best friend is the one who brings out the best in me."

—HENRY FORD

Well, I wasn't exactly bringing out the best in people. I was like one of those reverse magnets I learned how to make in science class. Instead of pulling people toward me, I was pushing them away. I knew that a lot of kids were only being nice to me because they were scared that if they weren't, I'd say bad things about them to other kids.

I've learned so much from Mrs. Petrowski about bullying . . . and myself. She's helped me become a better friend, and now I'm a lot happier. It's way more fun to be around kids who like you than kids who are scared of you.

Mrs. Petrowski always says,

I figure that the more information I can give you about bullying, the more POWER you'll have to choose friends you can trust and to be the kind of friend other kids want to hang out with.

HERE'S WHAT I DIDN'T KNOW ABOUT BULLYING

I used to think of bullying as only being physical—like when someone hurts your body on purpose.

But I was wrong. I've learned that there are other ways to bully.
And I used them.

I used my words . . .

You're sooooo sensitive

Hi, Mon-iCK-A!

You're Such a Loser!

. . . and sometimes, I'd be mean without using any words at all.

I'd laugh at
kids' mistakes.

I'd ignore them
on purpose.

And I'd make
faces at them.

I'd also tell friends what they could and couldn't do.

If you don't let me play with that ball, you can't come to my birthday party next week.

YOU CAN'T BE FRIENDS WITH HER IF YOU'RE FRIENDS WITH ME.

YOU CAN HANG OUT WITH US, BUT SHE CAN'T. SHE'S NOT COOL ENOUGH TO BE A PART OF OUR GROUP.

I'd be mean right in front of them . . .

THAT'S ONE UH-GLEE SHIRT. JUST KIDDING!

. . . and behind their backs.

Did you hear about Ana? She got a D on that easy math test. What a dummy! Pass it on.

Another kind of bullying is cyber-bullying. I didn't do it, but I found out there are lots of kids my age and older who do.

Kids who cyber-bully use the Internet, cell phones, cameras, text messaging, and stuff like that to hurt others.

They might send or text mean messages about someone . . .

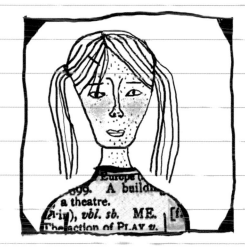

or take a really embarrassing picture of a kid and put it on a website for lots of people to see . . .

or start an online I-Hate-So-and-So Club and get other kids to say bad things about that person!

Bullying happens whenever someone hurts your body, your feelings, your reputation, or your friendships ON PURPOSE. And it happens a lot. I had no idea how big a problem bullying is until Mrs. Petrowski showed me this fact card:

WOW! BULLYING IS A BIG PROBLEM FOR KIDS!

Quick Facts

- Nine out of ten elementary students have been bullied by their peers.[1]
- The majority of eight- to eleven-year-olds—74 percent—said teasing and bullying occur at their schools.[2]
- Every day, 160,000 kids miss school because of bullying.[3]
- Kids are, on average, the targets of bullying about once every three to six minutes from the start of kindergarten to the end of first grade.[4]
- Eight-year-old kids who bully are six times more likely to be convicted of a crime by age twenty-four.[5]
- Most cyber-bullying occurs between nine and fourteen years of age.[6]
- More than half of all kids in grades four through eight—58 percent—have not told their parents or an adult of hurtful/mean things sent to them online.[7]

Studies listed in back of book.

Mrs. Petrowski said lots of kids who get bullied don't tell anyone about it because they're too embarrassed and scared to say anything. They think it'll make the problem worse. "Maybe it's better to pretend you're invisible and put up with it until the kid finds someone else to pick on," I told her.

Mrs. Petrowski sighed. I bet you can guess where she headed next. That's right. Over to her Think About It file. Here's the card she gave me:

THINK ABOUT IT

"One of the greatest diseases
is to be a nobody to somebody."

—MOTHER TERESA

Mother Teresa was right. Who wants to feel like a nobody?

I know I didn't like it when my sister gave me the silent treatment for a whole week because I borrowed her shirt without asking.

NOT ALL KIDS WHO BULLY LOOK LIKE BAD GUYS.

Take it from me—this is NOT what most bullying kids look like:

They can be boys or girls, and they come in all shapes, sizes, and ages.

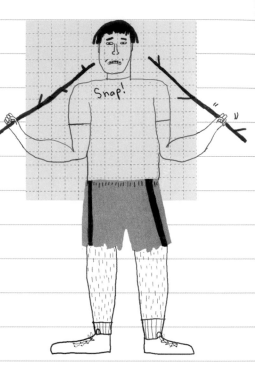

People who bully can even be grown-ups. (Sheesh! You would think older people would know better!)

Mrs. Petrowski says that younger kids who bully, if they don't get the help they need, turn into even meaner grown-ups.

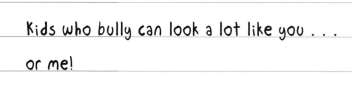

Kids who bully can look a lot like you . . . or me!

(This is me, by the way, writing this very important book!)

KIDS WHO GET BULLIED COULD BE ANYBODY!

Sure, some kids like to pick on anyone who looks, acts, thinks, talks, or dresses differently than they do. But they can also go after people who seem to be a lot like them.

Kids who get bullied (Mrs. Petrowski calls them the "targets" of bullying) can be boys or girls. And, just like the kids who bully, targets come in all shapes, sizes, and ages.

WHY DO KIDS BULLY?

I've heard a lot of excuses for being mean on purpose. I've even used some of these myself: Her clothes are so-o-o dorky.

She's such a nerd. **HE'S W-E-I-R-D.** HE'S SO GAY.

HE'S TOO FAT. SHE DOESN'T LOOK LIKE US. HE SMELLS. (P.U.!)

Mrs. Petrowski says there's really only ONE reason why people pick on others: It's because they're CHOOSING to be mean. It's as if they're putting on a bully hat, so that they can play the part of the bad guy who goes after the good guy—like in the movies.

Here's something I bet you'd be surprised to know: at one time or another, you may have worn that bully hat, just like me. WHAT? You don't believe me? Okay, then, be honest: when kids have been mean to you, have you ever been mean back—on purpose? See how easy it is to wear that hat?

The important thing to know about the bully hat is that you can choose to put it on or take it off. Like Mrs. Petrowski says, "The choice is all yours." Remember why I decided to take off my bully hat? I learned that bullying hurts everyone—including the kids who are bullying!

Quick Facts

- Bullying is a learned behavior. Kids can learn it at home, on the playground, in school, or in their neighborhood.[8]
- Kids find emotional bullying (spreading rumors, gossiping, giving the silent treatment, or excluding others from groups or activities) MORE HARMFUL than physical bullying![9]
- There's safety in numbers: it's harder for kids to bully you when you have supportive classmates by your side.[10]

Studies listed in back of book.

OUCH! BULLYING
HURSE EVERYONE

OUCH! BULLYING
HURTS EVERYONE

Quick Facts

- **TARGETS:** Kids who are bullied get headaches and stomachaches. They feel sad most of the time and don't want to go to school. They can also end up hurting themselves and others.
- **BYSTANDERS:** Kids who see other kids get bullied don't feel safe and get headaches and stomachaches, just like the kids who are being bullied! They feel helpless and powerless, and also have trouble coping with and solving problems.
- **BULLIES:** Kids who bully others are more likely to go to jail, use alcohol or drugs, have eating disorders, or drop out of school when they're older. They are also likely to feel lonely or sad and have fewer close friends.

NOBODY LIKES BEING TREATED BADLY. NOT EVEN THE KIDS WHO BULLY!

Mrs. Petrowski says that some kids DON'T like taking responsibility for their mean behavior. I know I didn't. I figured the kids I picked on somehow deserved it. I mean, was it really my problem that so-and-so was such a loser?

But a few weeks ago, something happened in class that got me thinking. Our teacher, Mr. Randall, had us practice out loud our lines from a play we're reading. When it was Javier's turn, he stuttered a lot. I knew he couldn't help it, but that didn't stop me from rolling my eyes and laughing. Mr. Randall looked mad. I thought he was going to give the same old, boring talk about how it's not nice to laugh and make fun of other kids. But he didn't. Instead, he told us about a new class rule: kids with freckles have to stay after class to clean up the classroom. What?! I thought. I've got freckles. That is SO not fair!

When the bell rang, I went to Mr. Randall to tell him what I thought about his stupid new rule. "Why do you think it's unfair?" he asked.

"Because it's not my fault I have freckles. They're just a part of who I am. I shouldn't be punished for that."

"Hmmm . . . ," said Mr. Randall. "That's a good point, Katie. Just like how Javier talks is a part of who he is. Should he be made fun of for who he is?"

"I guess not . . ."

Then Mr. Randall had me write down how I would describe myself to somebody who has never met me before. This is what I wrote:

WHO AM I?

My name is Katie McDonnell.

I'm almost 11 years old.

I'm tall and thin.

The color of my skin is white and I have freckles.

I have curly brown hair and green eyes.

I bite my nails when I get nervous.

I'm a good reader but I'm not good in math.

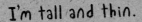

I showed Mr. Randall my list when I was done. "Now tell me," he said, "how would you feel if one of your classmates made fun of any of the items on your Who-Am-I list?"

Ouch! I never thought of it that way before.

I ended up apologizing to Javier because I knew it was the right thing to do. And I still had cleanup duty—not because of my freckles, Mr. Randall explained, but because that was the *consequence* for what I did to Javier. Sheesh! There was that word again. Every teacher in this school must use Mr. Sanders' dictionary!

THINK ABOUT IT

"Never be bullied into silence. Never allow yourself to be made a victim. Accept no one's definition of your life; define yourself."

—HARVEY FIERSTEIN

WHAT DO KIDS WHO BULLY WANT?

When I wore my bully hat, I wanted to push your buttons.

I wanted to make you **MAD**

I wanted to make you  Scared

I wanted to make you Sad

When I pushed your buttons, it made me feel more powerful than you. And I liked that feeling so much that I turned into a power-sucking machine—sucking all the power right out of you and putting it into me.

Don't let kids like me do that!

Power

Katie Power Vac 3000

Now I know this can be really hard to do. But you have more power than you think, without having to be mean back and make things worse.

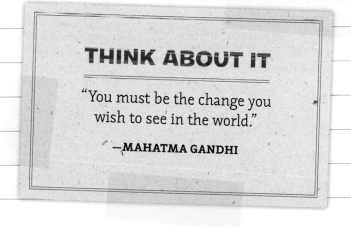

THINK ABOUT IT

"You must be the change you wish to see in the world."

—MAHATMA GANDHI

Mr. Gandhi sure sounds a lot like my grandma. She's always telling me, "Treat people the way you want to be treated."

But sometimes it's really hard to figure out how to treat someone who is hurting you with their words. That's where grown-ups can help.

Mrs. Petrowski says that everyone on this planet is born with a special tool belt. In fact, you're wearing yours right now, even though you can't see it or feel it.

If you could see it, I think this is what it would look like:

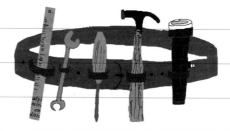

The problem is that the tools don't automatically come with our tool belts. Grown-ups need to give them to us. Sometimes, though, they forget or don't even know about these tools! But don't worry. Since I got my starter tool set from Mrs. Petrowski, I'll share mine with you.

INTRODUCING . . . MRS. PETROWSKI'S TOTALLY AWESOME EMPOWER TOOLS

I've practiced using these tools lots of times with Mrs. Petrowski, and they really do work!

Just last week, my brother called me a "freckle-faced dork" in front of his friends—including this boy I kind of like. How embarrassing is that? But instead of losing it by crying or yelling at him like I'd normally do, this is what I said:

You should have seen the surprised look on my brother's face. That felt so-o-o good! And the best part is that *I didn't have to be mean to feel good!*

Check out how to use these tools when someone says something mean like "you're fat" on purpose:

"Stop!"*
Look the kid in the eye and tell him to stop talking to you that way.

"Why? Why? Why?"
Ask a "why" question after someone says something mean to you. It distracts the kid who is trying to push your buttons.

Walk Away

If someone is being mean to you, you don't have to stand there and take it.

Walk or run to a safe place and hang out with grown-ups and kids you trust.

"So," "Whatever," "Huh," "Who cares?"

Say one or two words in a neutral tone. Make sure your words aren't cruel or hurtful.

Change the Subject

Distract the kid by talking calmly about other things.

Act Silly or Goofy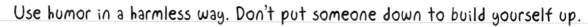

Use humor in a harmless way. Don't put someone down to build yourself up.

Turn an Insult into a Compliment*

Turn the negative into something positive— ONLY if it doesn't bother you to do this.

Agree*

Go along with what the kid says—ONLY if you don't feel bad doing this.

*IMPORTANT: If a tool doesn't work, don't keep using it. And if you don't feel comfortable or safe using any of the tools, like the Stop!, Turn-an-Insult-into-a-Compliment, or Agree tools, don't use them. Try another tool instead.

Have you noticed there's no Ignore tool? Many grown-ups give the advice, "Just ignore him and he'll eventually stop." So I've asked a bunch of kids if this advice worked for them. Some said yes, but most said no. I even think it can sometimes make the problem worse. When I wore the bully hat, I would work harder to push your buttons if you tried to ignore me!

These tools won't end all your bullying problems. And they won't stop kids from bullying other kids. That's why it's really important to report what happened to grown-ups you trust so they can make sure everyone gets the help and protection they need.

USE YOUR TOOLS FOR GOOD, NOT EVIL

The first four tools are better for little kids to use. Bigger kids like you and me can handle all eight tools. Act them out with people you trust, like your mom or dad, sister or brother, teacher, school counselor, or good friend. Have them pretend they're wearing the bully hat, so you can figure out what to say or do—without putting on a bully hat yourself. (This is what Mrs. Petrowski calls "role-play.")

HOW DO YOU DEAL WITH PHYSICAL BULLYING?

I've heard some parents tell their kids, "If someone hits you, hit him back." But Mrs. Petrowski says that hitting back or getting even is definitely NOT the answer. Why? Because it can make the problem much worse and lead to the use of weapons—and that's just really scary.

If someone tries to hurt your body, Mrs. Petrowski recommends getting away as fast as you can to a safe place, like the library, school office, or anywhere there are grown-ups or a bunch of friends who can protect and support you. "Also, look into signing up for a self-defense class so you can protect yourself from the person attacking you," she adds.

WHAT CAN YOU DO IF SOMEONE IS CYBER-BULLYING YOU?

If you get a hurtful email, text message, or anything like that, don't get even by sending a mean message back. If you do, you'll be cyber-bullying too! And you can get in A LOT of trouble wearing that cyber bully hat—not just with your parents (who could ground you for a trillion years) but also with your school, and even the police. It's much better to save the message, print it out if you can, and show it to a grown-up you trust. That teacher, parent, or school counselor needs to know what's happening in order to protect you.

IF YOU'RE BEING BULLIED OR SEE SOMEONE BEING BULLIED, TELL A GROWN-UP YOU TRUST.

I used to think that the kids who saw me being mean to Monica on the playground were snitches—tattling to the playground monitor just to get me in trouble. But I was wrong. They were trying to help Monica get out of trouble. Whenever you're dealing with bullying, it's ALL about reporting.

Here's an example of me tattling:

"M-O-M! JENNA ATE SOME COOKIES WHEN YOU TOLD US NO SWEETS UNTIL AFTER DINNER!"

This is Jenna sticking out her tongue at me because I tattled on her.

HOW RUDE!

Here's an example of me reporting:

"M-O-M! MIKE'S SITTING ON JENNA AND SHE CAN'T GET AWAY.
JENNA'S CRYING. SHE NEEDS HELP!"

This is Jenna sharing her cookie with me because I came to her rescue.

YUM!

Quick Facts

Know the Difference between Tattling & Reporting

- **TATTLING** is when you're trying to get kids IN trouble when they aren't hurting themselves or others. That's something you DON'T want to do. It will not help you make or keep friends.

- **REPORTING** is when you're trying to help kids OUT of trouble because they're getting hurt. That's something you DO want to do. Bullying is abuse. Report bullying to a grown-up you trust. If no one listens or takes your problem seriously, keep reporting until you find a grown-up who does.

WHAT ELSE CAN YOU DO TO HELP KIDS WHO ARE BEING BULLIED?

One thing for sure, if you're the bystander (the kid who sees other kids getting hurt), it's not good to ignore it. When this girl on my swim team was bullying me, most of my teammates did nothing; some even laughed at that girl's mean jokes. It felt like they were joining her team—the bullying team. I was so hurt that my friends didn't stick up for me that I went to Mrs. Petrowski's office to talk to her about it.

THINK ABOUT IT

"In the end, we will remember not the words of our enemies, but the silence of our friends."

—DR. MARTIN LUTHER KING, JR.

"I get what Dr. King is saying," I told Mrs. Petrowski. "But what if the bystander doesn't feel safe saying 'Cut it out!' because there's a really good chance the mean kid will come after her?"

"Well," she explained, "there is more than one way to help—without risking your own safety." And that's when Mrs. Petrowski went over this "Be a Hero Bystander" list with me:

BE A HERO BYSTANDER

Notice it and care.

Imagine what it would be like to be in the shoes of the kid who is being bullied. How would you feel? Caring is the first step on the road to helping.

STeLLar

Tell the kid who is bullying to stop—only if you feel safe.

It's best to confront him when there are other kids around to support you, or if he's smaller and younger than you. If it's too risky or scary for you to do, get help from an adult you trust.

Reach out to kids who are being bullied.

Listen to their concerns and comfort them. Include them in your group or activity. Support them when the bullying takes place or afterwards in private. Let them know that NO ONE deserves to be treated that way.

Don't join the bullying team.

If you laugh or smile at other people's putdowns, you're letting them know that it's okay to be cruel. And if you do nothing while or after the bullying takes place, you're sending the message that the target somehow deserves it. Don't encourage bullying by laughing, clapping, spreading a nasty rumor, or joining in. Be a part of the solution, not a part of the problem.

Report bullying to a grown-up you trust.

Go to someone who will not let the kid who is bullying know it was you who reported the bullying. That way, everyone can get the help, support, AND protection they need.

"LOOK, UP IN THE SKY!
IT'S THE HERO BYSTANDER!"

WHAT MAKES A FRIEND A GOOD FRIEND?

Have you ever noticed there's always some kid at school who says she's your friend but doesn't really act like it? I have. I've even told Mrs. Petrowski about this girl in my P.E. class who's sweet and nice to me in front of my face and then says really mean things about me behind my back.

"Hmmm...," she said, "that sounds a lot like what had happened between you and Monica."

Sheesh! I didn't realize I did the same thing to Monica. Now I know how she felt.

> ## THINK ABOUT IT
>
> "We often focus on the mean things others do to us, without really paying attention to the mean things we're doing to others."
>
> **—MRS. PETROWSKI**

Quick Facts

Bystanders Can Make a Positive Difference

- About 80 percent of bullying on elementary school playgrounds has an audience.
- When bystanders do intervene, they can stop the bullying about 50 percent of the time.[11]

Studies listed in back of book.

To help me understand how to be a better friend, Mrs. Petrowski gave me this friendship chart:

GOOD FRIENDS	BAD FRIENDS
. . . appreciate and like you for who you are.	. . . put you down to build themselves up.
. . . accept that you get to choose your own friends.	. . . tell you who you can be friends with.
. . . make you feel welcome in their group or activity.	. . . won't let you join their group or activity.
. . . have good things to say about you to their friends.	. . . gossip, spread rumors, or send hurtful email and text messages about you.
. . . use humor in a harmless way.	. . . hide behind the words "just kidding" or "no offense, but . . ." when saying something really hurtful.
. . . make you feel accepted and safe.	. . . make you feel unaccepted and unsafe.
. . . work things out with you when you have problems.	. . . refuse to admit when they did something wrong and they keep doing it!
. . . are friends you can count on, every day.	. . . are nice one day and mean the next.
. . . really want to hang out with you.	. . . only play with you until "someone better" comes along.

I've started thinking back on some of the things I did to Monica:

I wouldn't let her play wall ball with me and Sarah.
I whispered about her to other girls—in front of her and behind her back.
I even made fun of her.

How I treated Monica didn't exactly put me on the Good Friends side of this list. No wonder she doesn't want to have anything to do with me anymore. And I can't say that I blame her. In fact, I'd be surprised if she'd ever want to talk to me again.

I realize I'm not going to be good friends with everyone. Nobody is. But I am trying harder to treat the kids at school and in my neighborhood in a more respectful, friendly way.

Sometimes I still mess up by saying and doing stupid things. Mrs. Petrowski says that since people aren't perfect, you can't expect friendships to be perfect. "We all make mistakes," she explained. "The important thing is to learn from our mistakes so that we don't keep repeating them."

I know I can't change what I did in the past. But I can change what I do from now on.

When I told this to Mrs. Petrowski, she gave me a big bear hug.

Not everyone is lucky enough to have a Mrs. Petrowski at their school. But I bet there's someone you can talk to if you've got a bullying problem. Don't be afraid to ask for help. If you do, then maybe more of those stinky old bully hats will end up in the garbage—where they belong!

Dear Monica—

I am really sorry that I was so mean to you and spread nasty rumors about you. Those weren't nice things to do. You didn't deserve it. I don't know if you will ever be able to forgive me. I just wanted you to know how sorry I am. I promise I won't do that to you or anyone else again.

Sincerely,
Katie

Author's Note to Parents & Teachers

"It is our choices that show what we truly are, far more than our abilities."

—J.K. ROWLING

Confessions of a Former Bully is the culmination of what I've learned over the years about bullying to help empower young children to make good choices in life. It is also a call to action for caring adults to step up and make a positive difference in the lives of targets, bystanders, and aggressors.

Back in the days when I was an elementary student, bullying research was quite limited, and our schools and government sorely lacked constructive methods of addressing aggression. For countless children, a typical day in the schoolyard basically played out like a scene from *Lord of the Flies*. But times are changing. We now have extensive, concrete evidence of the long-term, damaging effects of physical, verbal, and relational aggression. And many U.S. schools are being held legally accountable for their mishandling of bullying incidents. Efforts are also under way to tackle the growing epidemic of cyber-bullying—the use of the Internet and other communication devices to intentionally hurt others.

CREATING SAFER SCHOOL CLIMATES

For an anti-bullying program to be truly effective in a school, aggression must be consistently addressed from classroom to classroom; on the playground and school buses; as well as in the cafeteria, gym, bathrooms, and hallways. Numerous experts stress the importance of implementing a systematic, school-wide approach that:

- raises community awareness about bullying among school staff, students, and parents
- promotes effective nonviolent strategies to address bullying
- develops clear rules against bullying and enforces those rules in a consistent manner
- maintains a positive emotional tone between youth and adult
- employs predictable and escalating consequences for aggression
- provides aggressors with opportunities for restitution
- empowers bystanders to support the target and discourage the bullying
- protects targets and bystanders from further retaliation by aggressors
- follows up to ensure bullying is not continuing

Stan Davis's books *Schools Where Everyone Belongs: Practical Strategies for Reducing Bullying* and *Empowering Bystanders in Bullying Prevention* are excellent resources exploring what works and doesn't work in elementary schools. Also refer to recommended resources for more helpful information.

Today's children are tomorrow's leaders. We need to encourage them to care and respond to the injustices they see. In so doing, we continue to lay the groundwork for a more just and compassionate society.

Trudy Ludwig

Recommended Resources

ORGANIZATIONS

Committee for Children
568 First Avenue South, Suite 600
Seattle, WA 98104
www.cfchildren.org

Girls Inc.
120 Wall Street
New York, NY 10005-3902
www.girlsinc.org

Hands & Words Are Not for Hurting Project
PO Box 2644
Salem, OR 97308-2644
www.handsproject.org

International Bullying Prevention Association (IBPA)
www.stopbullyingworld.com

National Crime Prevention Council
2345 Crystal Drive, Suite 500
Arlington, VA 22202
www.ncpc.org/topics/bullying

Operation Respect
2 Penn Plaza, 5th Floor
New York, NY 10121
www.operationrespect.org

The Ophelia Project®
718 Nevada Drive
Erie, PA 16505
www.opheliaproject.org

WEBSITES

www.bullying.org
This informative website for adults and children includes anti-bullying commercials, drawings, stories, music, and films. It also allows users to share experiences with others who have witnessed and been involved in bullying.

www.cyberbully.org
Created by the Center for Safe and Responsible Internet Use, this website offers students, parents, and educators valuable information and resources for combating online social cruelty.

www.eyesonbullying.org
Created by the Education Development Center, this website is both informative and user-friendly. Check out their wonderful Toolkit, in PDF format, which includes insights, strategies, activities, and resources to address bullying for caregivers, parents, and youth.

www.isafe.org
iSAFE America, Inc., a nonprofit foundation endorsed by the U.S. Congress, provides information to educate and empower students to use the Internet safely.

www.netsmartz.org
This interactive educational resource is provided by the National Center for Missing & Exploited Children and Boys & Girls Clubs of America. It addresses a variety of Internet safety issues for kids ages five to seventeen, parents, guardians, educators, and law enforcement officers.

www.stopbullyingnow.com
Founded by anti-bullying expert Stan Davis, this website contains practical research-based strategies to reduce bullying in schools.

www.stopbullyingnow.hrsa.gov/index.asp
This is the federal government's interactive anti-bullying website for kids and adults to learn more about bullying and what can be done to address it.

www.teachingtolerance.org
Founded by the Southern Poverty Law Center, this site is a wonderful resource for school educators and administrators interested in reducing prejudice, improving intergroup relations, and fostering respect for differences among children.

www.wiredsafety.org
Founded by Internet privacy and security attorney Parry Aftab, this website is a great cyber-bullying resource for parents, educators, and kids.

BOOKS FOR ADULTS

Borba, Michele, Ed.D. *Nobody Likes Me, Everybody Hates Me: The Top 25 Friendship Problems and How to Solve Them.* San Francisco: Jossey-Bass, 2005.

Coloroso, Barbara. *The Bully, the Bullied, and the Bystander.* New York: HarperResource, 2003.

Davis, Stan. *Empowering Bystanders in Bullying Prevention.* Champaign: Research Press, 2007.

Davis, Stan. *Schools Where Everyone Belongs: Practical Strategies for Reducing Bullying.* Champaign: Research Press, 2005.

Dellasega, Cheryl, Ph.D., and Charisse Nixon, Ph.D. *Girl Wars: 12 Strategies That Will End Female Bullying.* New York: Simon & Schuster, 2003.

Freedman, Judy S. *Easing the Teasing: Helping Your Child Cope with Name-Calling, Ridicule, and Verbal Bullying.* New York: McGraw-Hill/Contemporary Books, 2002.

Garbarino, James. *And Words Can Hurt Forever: How to Protect Adolescents from Bullying, Harassment, and Emotional Violence.* New York: Free Press, 2003.

Olweus, Dan. *Bullying at School: What We Know and What We Can Do.* Malden: Wiley-Blackwell, 1993.

Rigby, Ken. *Children and Bullying: How Parents and Educators Can Reduce Bullying at School.* Malden: Wiley-Blackwell, 2008.

Simmons, Rachel. *Odd Girl Out: The Hidden Culture of Aggression in Girls.* New York: Harcourt, 2002.

Thompson, Michael, Lawrence J. Cohen, and Catherine O'Neill Grace. *Best Friends, Worst Enemies: Understanding the Social Lives of Children.* New York: Ballantine Books, 2001.

Thompson, Michael, Lawrence J. Cohen, and Catherine O'Neill Grace. *Mom, They're Teasing Me: Helping Your Child Solve Social Problems.* New York: Ballantine Books, 2002.

Willard, Nancy. *Cyberbullying and Cyberthreats.* Champaign: Research Press, 2007.

Willard, Nancy. *Cyber-Safe Kids, Cyber-Savvy Teens.* San Francisco: Jossey-Bass, 2007.

Wiseman, Rosalind. *Queen Bees & Wannabees: Helping Your Daughter Survive Cliques, Gossip, Boyfriends & Other Realities of Adolescence.* New York: Crown, 2002.

BOOKS FOR KIDS

Burnett, Karen Gedig. *Simon's Hook: A Story about Teases and Putdowns.* Roseville: GR Publishing, 2002.

Carlson, Nancy. *How to Lose All Your Friends.* New York: Puffin, 1997.

Codell, Esmé Raji. *Vive La Paris.* New York: Hyperion, 2007.

Criswell, Patti Kelley. *Friends: Making Them & Keeping Them.* Middleton: American Girl, 2006.

Criswell, Patti Kelley. *Stand Up for Yourself & Your Friends.* Middleton: American Girl, 2009.

DePino, Catherine. *Blue Cheese Breath and Stinky Feet.* Washington, D.C.: Magination Press, 2004.

Estes, Eleanor. *The Hundred Dresses.* New York: Scholastic, 1973.

Gervay, Susanne. *I Am Jack.* Berkeley: Tricycle Press, 2009.

Hoose, Phillip, and Hannah Hoose. *Hey, Little Ant.* Berkeley: Tricycle Press, 1998.

Humphrey, Sandra McLeod. *Hot Issues, Cool Choices: Facing Bullies, Peer Pressure, Popularity, and Putdowns.* New York: Prometheus Books, 2007.

Kaufman, Gershen, Ph.D., et al. *Stick Up for Yourself! Every Kid's Guide to Personal Power and Positive Self-Esteem.* Minneapolis: Free Spirit Publishing, 1999.

Ludwig, Trudy. *Just Kidding.* Berkeley: Tricycle Press, 2006.

Ludwig, Trudy. *My Secret Bully.* Berkeley: Tricycle Press, 2005.

Ludwig, Trudy. *Sorry!* Berkeley: Tricycle Press, 2006.

Ludwig, Trudy. *Too Perfect.* Berkeley: Tricycle Press, 2009.

Ludwig, Trudy. *Trouble Talk®.* Berkeley: Tricycle Press, 2008.

Madonna. *Mr. Peabody's Apples.* New York: Callaway, 2003.

Moss, Peggy. *Our Friendship Rules.* Gardiner: Tilbury House, 2007.

Moss, Peggy. *Say Something.* Gardiner: Tilbury House, 2004.

Romain, Trevor. *Bullies Are a Pain in the Brain.* Minneapolis: Free Spirit Publishing, 1997.

Romain, Trevor. *Cliques, Phonies, & Other Baloney.* Minneapolis: Free Spirit Publishing, 1998.

Spinelli, Jerry. *Crash.* New York: Dell Yearling, 1996.

STUDIES CITED

1. Stanford University School of Medicine & Lucile Packard Children's Hospital, 2007
2. Kaiser Family Foundation & Nickelodeon, 2001
3. National Education Association, 1995
4. The Center for the Advancement of Health, 2003
5. Maine Project Against Bullying, 2000
6. WiredSafety.org
7. iSAFE America, 2004
8. National Association of School Psychologists, 2003
9. Galen & Underwood, 1997; Werner & Hill, 2003
10. Davis, *Empowering Bystanders*, 2007
11. LaMarsh Report, 2000

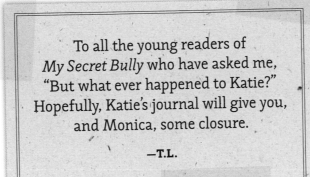

To all the young readers of
My Secret Bully who have asked me,
"But what ever happened to Katie?"
Hopefully, Katie's journal will give you,
and Monica, some closure.

—T.L.

Text copyright © 2010 by Trudy Ludwig
Cover and interior illustrations copyright © 2010 by Beth Adams

All rights reserved. Published in the United States by Dragonfly Books, an imprint of Random House Children's Books, a division of Random House, Inc., New York. Originally published in hardcover in the United States by Tricycle Press, an imprint of Random House Children's Books, New York, in 2010.

Dragonfly Books with the colophon is a registered trademark of Random House, Inc.

Visit us on the Web! randomhouse.com/kids

Educators and librarians, for a variety of teaching tools, visit us at randomhouse.com/teachers

The Library of Congress has cataloged the hardcover edition of this work as follows:
Ludwig, Trudy.
Confessions of a former bully / by Trudy Ludwig ; illustrated by Beth Adams. — 1st ed.
p. cm.
Summary: Ten-year-old Katie's consequences for bullying classmates include making up for the hurt she has caused, and so she decides to write a book about bullying, why it is not okay, and how to start being a better friend.
ISBN 978-1-58246-309-4 (trade) — ISBN 978-1-58246-358-2 (lib. bdg.)
[1. Bullies—Fiction. 2. Schools—Fiction. 3. Behavior—Fiction. 4. Authorship—Fiction.] I. Adams, Beth, ill. II. Title.
PZ7.L9763Con 2010
[Fic]—dc22
2009032296

ISBN 978-0-307-93113-9 (pbk.)

MANUFACTURED IN CHINA

12

First Dragonfly Books Edition

Random House Children's Books supports the First Amendment and celebrates the right to read.